A JIGSAW JONES MYSTERY

The Case of the Haunted Scarecrow

Read more Jigsaw Jones Mysteries by James Preller

The Case from Outer Space—New!

The Case of the Hat Burglar—New!

The Case of the Smelly Sneaker

The Case of the Bicycle Bandit

The Case of the Glow-in-the-Dark Ghost

The Case of the Mummy Mystery

The Case of the Best Pet Ever

The Case of the Buried Treasure

The Case of the Disappearing Dinosaur

The Case of the Million-Dollar Mystery

The Case of the Bear Scare

The Case of the Golden Key

The Case of the Vanishing Painting

A JIGSAW JONES MYSTERY

The Case of the Haunted Scarecrow

by James Preller

illustrated by Jamie Smith
cover illustration by R. W. Alley

FEIWEL AND FRIENDS
New York

A FEIWEL AND FRIENDS BOOK
An imprint of Macmillan Publishing Group, LLC
120 Broadway, New York, NY 10271

Our books may be purchased in bulk for promotional, educational, or business
use. Please contact your local bookseller or the Macmillan Corporate and
Premium Sales Department at (800) 221-7945 ext. 5442 or by email at
MacmillanSpecialMarkets@macmillan.com.

Library of Congress Cataloging-in-Publication Data is available.

ISBN 978-1-250-20764-7 (paperback) / ISBN 978-1-250-20763-0 (ebook)

Book design by Véronique Lefèvre Sweet

Illustrations by Jamie Smith

Feiwel and Friends logo designed by Filomena Tuosto

First Feiwel and Friends edition, 2019

Originally published by Scholastic in 2001

Art used with permission from Scholastic

1   3   5   7   9   10   8   6   4   2

mackids.com

For Mags,
you've got a great smile, kid.

CONTENTS

Chapter 1

Leaves

Every fall my dad makes us rake the yard, front and back. He calls it "The Big Fall Cleanup."

I call it something else.

Yeesh.

My oldest brother, Billy, wasn't around to help. He worked weekends at the gas station. And my sister, Hillary, was like a magician. If there was work to do—*poof!*—she disappeared. That left me and my brothers Daniel and Nick.

I leaned against my rake and groaned. "How come we always get the dirty work?"

"Almost done, boys," my dad hollered from the front stoop, a newspaper open on his lap. He enjoyed watching us work. Rags sat beside him, slobbering cheerfully. Rags liked watching us work, too.

The lazy furball.

"Me and Nick are starting a leaf-raking business," Daniel told my dad.

"Oh?"

"Yeah," Nick chimed in. "We put up flyers and everything."

"Good for you," my dad said. "But you've got competition. Buzzy Lennon has most of the neighborhood all signed up."

"Buzzy's a rip-off artist!" Daniel exclaimed. "His prices are *way* too high. I heard he charged poor old Mrs. Rigby a hundred dollars last year."

"Buzzy's a thief," Nick claimed. "That's why we're gonna steal his business!"

He smiled like a fox.

Then he pushed Daniel into a leaf pile. Daniel turned and tackled Nick around the legs. Naturally, I joined in. That was probably a mistake. Daniel and Nick were stronger than me. Pretty soon I was getting the worst of it.

I felt like an ant at a square dance. *Squish, squish,* if you know what I mean.

Buzz, buzz. Daniel pulled a phone from his back pocket. He glanced at the message and frowned. "That's weird."

"Put that phone down," Nick said to Daniel. "I need help stuffing this scarecrow."

I squirmed while Nick kneeled on my chest. He shoved crispy leaves down my shirt.

"Time out for second," Daniel declared. "Jigsaw, do you know a girl named Kim Lewis?"

"She's in my class," I said.

Daniel glanced down at his phone. "Well, I just got a text from her sister, Kayla. She says that Kim needs a detective. The famous

Jigsaw Jones, world-famous detective and scarecrow!"

Nick rolled off my chest, though I could tell it broke his heart. I rose to my feet. *Crunch, crackle.* A few leaves had found their way inside my underwear. I staggered to Daniel, rustling and crackling with each step. "Let me borrow your phone," I said. "These mysteries don't solve themselves."

The Client

I climbed up to my tree house. Ten feet off the ground, it was where I did all my Big Thinking. I sat down (*crunch*, *crackle*) and spoke into the phone, "Jigsaw Jones, private eye."

"Jigsaw?! This is Kim Lewis from Ms. Gleason's class. I need your help."

I told her she had called the right place. For a dollar a day, I made problems go away.

We talked briefly. Kim mentioned a stolen necklace. She talked about a mysterious note. We decided to meet at her house. An hour later, I'd washed my face, combed my hair, eaten lunch, and changed my underwear. Now I could walk without itching.

Mila Yeh was waiting outside. We'd been friends since forever. Maybe longer. Mila was also my partner. We ran the best detective agency in the school.

"So what's this about?" Mila asked.

"It's about a stolen necklace," I replied.

Mila whistled. "Sounds like a mystery to me."

Softly, Mila began to sing. Nothing new there. Mila was always singing something. She liked taking regular old songs and making up brand-new words. I recognized the tune. It was the "glory, glory" song, called "The Battle Hymn of the Republic." Instead of the word *Hallelujah*, she sang *Kimmy Lewis*.

"Glory, glory, Kimmy Lewis!
What's the story, Kimmy Lewis?
What's the story, Kimmy Lewis?
We need the facts right now!"

I interrupted Mila to point out a flyer on a tree.

LEAVE THE LEAVES TO US!

If you don't like 'em coming,
You'll love 'em LEAVING!
We're like birds, CHEAP, CHEAP,
CHEAP!!!

Call Daniel or Nick: 555-4523

"That's the third one so far," I commented. "Wow, my brothers really plastered the neighborhood."

Something caught Mila's attention. She slowed to a stop. "Look, it's the Rigby place." Mila pointed at a large gray house. It was badly in need of repairs. Paint peeled and shutters banged. The lawn was thick with leaves and weeds. A group of trees stood before us, with bare branches swaying in the wind. "Spooky, huh?" Mila murmured.

An old woman lived there. Too frail and alone to keep up with the chores.

Creeeak. An old tree groaned in the wind.

"Hey, a scarecrow," Mila noticed. The scarecrow was propped up in a lawn chair, staring out through pumpkiny eyes. It sat in the front yard, near a thicket of overgrown bushes. It wore blue jeans and a flannel shirt.

In fact, it was dressed better than me.

A long, low howl came from a nearby house. Then another: *A-oooooo, a-oooooo.*

"Let's go," I told Mila. "This place creeps me out."

Mila stared at the scarecrow, then back at the silent house. She twirled her long black hair, lost in thought. "I wonder how that got there," Mila murmured.

"Hello? Earth to Mila?" I interrupted. "Come on already. Kim lives around the corner."

Kim met us at the front door. She had short hair and neat, straight teeth. Three freckles danced on the tip of her nose. People said that Kim Lewis was cute as a button. I didn't know about that. I'd never seen a cute button before.

"I've been a mess since I found the note," Kim admitted. "My sister Kayla suggested I call you."

I chewed on that fact for a while. It was like cafeteria food. I had a hard time swallowing it. Kayla Lewis was in middle school with my brother Daniel. And, to be honest, I was surprised she recommended me.

I didn't think she knew my name.

Go figure.

"Can we see the note?" Mila asked.

Kim led us into her bedroom. She lifted a sheet of paper off her dresser. "I found it this morning."

I read the note:

> We have your necklace.
> If you want it back,
> Do what we tell you.
> We'll contact you soon.

"We, huh?" I said.

Kim looked at me.

"Not a one-person job," I noted. "*We* means two or more."

Chapter 3

The Ransom Note

"The note is typewritten," I observed.

"Probably done on a home computer," Mila concluded. "It's perfect. The punctuation is correct. No spelling mistakes."

I smirked. "At least we know Bobby Solofsky isn't behind this. He can't spell!"

"Why would you suspect him?" Kim asked.

"Everyone is a suspect," I told Kim, "especially Bobby Solofsky. He's been a stone in my shoe for years."

"A stone?"

"It's like a pain in the neck," I explained. "Only lower."

I scribbled in my detective journal.

"Where did you find the note?" I questioned.

"It was sticking out from under my jewelry box," Kim answered.

I picked up the box. "Mind if I look?"

Kim shrugged. "Sure."

The box was filled with jewelry. Most of it was cheap plastic. There were also some shells, a few rocks, and a couple hair clips.

"Most of that jewelry is play stuff," Kim explained. "You know, for dress-up. I kept the necklace in there."

"Was anything else taken?" Mila asked.

"No," Kim answered. "Just the necklace."

"Really?" I was surprised. "This necklace, was it worth a lot of money?"

Kim blinked, long and slow. She twisted her mouth into a smile. Kim was trying to put on a brave face—and doing a pretty good

job of it, too. She answered, "Not really valuable, I guess. It was just fake pearls, you know, nothing expensive. But . . ."

"But what?" Mila asked.

Kim touched her bare neck. "The necklace was a gift from my grandmother. And, you know, she died about a year ago. So I guess it means a lot to me." Kim glanced around the room. She suddenly seemed lost and confused. Like she didn't know where to turn. Then, to my surprise, she turned to me. Her words barely broke a whisper. "That necklace is like a memory, Jigsaw. A memory I don't want to lose."

She paused. "I *want* it back."

I'd seen that same look on other clients. Kim was counting on me. That's the way it is when you're a detective. You're the guy who is supposed to make everything right. And for a dollar a day, you do the best you can.

Chapter 4

The Mysterious Caller

"What should I do now?" Kim asked.

"Do what the note tells you to do," I said. "Sit back and wait."

"That's it?" Kim moaned. "Sit and wait?!"

Kim looked out the window, as if expecting the thieves to ring her doorbell.

I tried to sound patient and calm. "Listen to me, Kim. This looks like a ransom note. Know what that means?"

Kim settled on the edge of the bed. "Yes," she sighed. "They'll want money."

"Probably," I stated. "We won't know for sure until the thief contacts you again."

Mila added, "Most likely you'll get a call. The thieves will want to arrange a drop-off, a secret place to leave the money."

"I don't have a phone," Kim said.

"They'll find a way," I said. "Bad guys always do."

Kim nodded, looking solemn and worried.

I wiggled two fingers. "The way I figure it, you have two choices. First you could refuse to play ball. Ignore the note. Don't accept any messages. Hire us . . . and maybe we can get your necklace back."

"*Maybe?*" Kim echoed.

"No promises," I said. "No guarantees."

"What's my second choice?"

"You do what they ask," I said. "If they want money, you pay it. It's the surest way to get your necklace back. Think it over." I stretched my arms and yawned. "Meanwhile, do you have any spare grape juice? I'm as dry as the Sahara."

Kim brought in a tall stack of Pringles and three glasses of ginger ale. I wrote the word SUSPECTS in my journal. "Can you think of anyone who *might* have taken your necklace?" I inquired.

Kim shook her head.

Mila placed a hand on Kim's arm. She said in soft tones, "We'll need a list of anyone who could have gotten into your room. Friends *and* family."

Kim chewed on her lower lip. "I've got two older sisters and a younger brother. Kayla, Kelly, and Kyle," she said. "Danika slept over yesterday . . ."

"Danika Starling?" Mila asked.

Kim's eyes narrowed. "Yeah, she's here all the time."

I glanced at Mila. Danika was in our class. "Does Danika know where you keep your jewelry?" I questioned.

"Of course," Kim answered sharply. "But you don't think . . ."

I held out my hands. "Look, Kim. I'm a detective. I keep asking questions until I like the answers."

Kim's face flushed red. "Well, don't ask questions about Danika. She would never, ever steal from me!"

We sat in silence. The room darkened as daylight turned to dusk outside the window. A sudden rap on the door startled us. "Kimmy, telephone!" a female voice announced.

"Who is it, Kayla?" Kim shouted at the door.

"He didn't say," Kayla screamed back. "And I didn't ask."

We followed Kim into the kitchen. I heard footsteps clomping up the stairs. Kayla, I guessed. I glanced out the kitchen window. A white mountain bike with red front forks was locked beside an apple tree in the backyard. It was a Schwinn Moab 3—a very cool bike. I wished it were mine.

Kim picked up the phone. "Hello? Hello? Is anyone . . . ?" She fell silent.

Mila placed her ear near the receiver, trying to listen in. After a minute, Kim spoke.

"Yes, yes. The leaning oak. Penny Lane. By the Rigby house. Uh-huh. Now?!"

Kim turned to us, a look of surprise on her face. "He hung up."

"*He*?" I echoed. "Are you sure?"

Kim nodded. She was sure.

"I heard a giggle in the background," Mila added. "A girl, I think."

"A giggle, huh. I guess they think this is a joke," I said. "Well, I'm not laughing. What did the voice want?"

"You," Kim replied.

"Me?"

"Yes." Kim nodded. "You, Jigsaw."

Chapter
5

The Scarecrow

"They want *you* to deliver the money," Kim said.

And that was that. In one swoop, I went from detective to delivery boy. I was supposed to go to a tree, put three dollars in a hole, and leave. The voice said he'd return the necklace after I made the drop-off.

"I don't get it," Mila complained. "Why Jigsaw? How did they know he was here?"

"They must be watching the house," I concluded. "I doubt it's a one-person job. You heard giggles on the phone, remember."

Mila remembered.

Kim shivered—and not because the house was drafty. She ran her fingers across the front of her neck. It was a habit. She was feeling for a necklace that wasn't there.

"Let's do this," I declared.

Kim went to her room. She returned with four dollars. One for me. Three for the ransom. "You better hurry," she said. "They want you there right away."

I didn't like it. But I didn't have to like it. It was a job. Like raking leaves or selling lemonade. So off I went, into the dusky night. Mila stayed behind to keep Kim company.

I walked down Abbey Road. The evening chill nibbled on my ears like a pet parakeet. I turned right onto Penny Lane. The night was brisk and gloomy. I noticed that someone had ripped down one of my brothers' leaf-raking signs.

I came to the leaning oak tree. Its long branches reached out over the sidewalk. I shoved my hands into my pockets. There was no one in sight. But I had a perfect view of the Rigby place across the street.

A black cat slinked across the lawn.

There was one lonely light on in the old house. I may have glimpsed a shadow drift behind a curtain, then disappear. In that gloom, even the trees seemed lonely. Their leafless branches looked like twisted arms, the twigs like crippled fingers. I flicked up the collar of my jacket. A dog howled.

A-ooooo. A-ooooo.

I looked into the night sky. There was no moon. Just the pale yellow of distant stars. Well, it was time to finish the job. I soon found a small hollow in the tree. The kind of hole where a chipmunk or snake might hide. I peeked inside.

And there it was.

The necklace.

I pulled the three dollars from my pocket. I hesitated, the money still in my hand.

It made no sense. Why should I pay the robbers when I already had the necklace?

And why was the necklace here?

I didn't have time to answer my own questions.

I heard a noise. Maybe it was a faint whisper, or the scraping of a shoe on cement. Maybe a flashlight flickered, then died.

For whatever reason, I looked toward the Rigby place.

What I saw made my heart stop.

The scarecrow on Mrs. Rigby's lawn was standing. Staring straight at me. It was . . . *alive*.

I pressed myself against the tree. If I breathed, it was by accident. The scarecrow moved stiffly, as if waking from a long sleep.

First one step, then another. Like a mummy.
Or a living zombie.

Coming toward me.

Step by step.

I squeezed my eyes tight, trying to shut
away the fear. But when I opened them, the
creature was coming closer. Ever closer.

I clutched Kim's necklace in my hand.

And ran.

Chapter 6

Bad for Business

I called Kim's house the moment I got home. "I've got your necklace," I told her.

Kim was thrilled. Mila, on the other hand, was not. She didn't understand why I didn't return to Kim's house. "Now I have to walk home alone," Mila complained.

"No! Don't," I warned her. "Call your father. Get a ride. But do not—I repeat, DO NOT—walk home alone. It's too dangerous."

"Dangerous? What's going on, Jigsaw?" Mila asked. "You sound strange."

"Just promise me," I urged, "you won't walk home alone."

Mila groaned. And grumbled. And, finally, promised.

"Good," I said with relief. "I'll explain it all tomorrow."

I didn't say much during dinner. Not that anyone cared. At my house, there's always somebody yapping—usually Grams. She

talks so much, Grams has to give her teeth a rest. And she does! Every night she leaves them in a glass jar with fizzing bubbles. In the morning Grams pops her teeth back in and starts chattering all over again.

Like Dad says, "Grams gives those choppers a workout!"

Grams moved in with us when I was four, back when Grandpa passed away. I loved listening to her stories, especially tonight. It almost took my mind off the scarecrow.

Almost.

I knocked on Daniel and Nick's bedroom door after dinner. Nick lounged on the top bunk, reading *Ghost* by Jason Reynolds. Daniel was studying his bankbook, adding numbers on a piece of paper. "What's up, Worm?" he said.

I plopped on the floor, cross-legged. "You won't believe what happened to me."

I was right. They didn't believe me.

"Well, paint me blue and call me a Smurf," Nick scoffed. "Jigsaw's lost his marbles."

Daniel just laughed. Then he looked at me closely. "You're serious, aren't you?"

I was dead serious.

Nick jumped down to the floor. "Tell us again," he demanded. So I did.

My brothers still looked doubtful. But I made them promise. "Don't go near the Rigby place," I insisted. "Promise me. It's too dangerous."

Daniel rolled his eyes toward the ceiling. Nick frowned. "Okay," Daniel finally agreed. "If it means that much to you, Worm. It's too bad, though. Old Mrs. Rigby pays top dollar. We were hoping to get her business."

Nick said, "Well, money's not everything. When it comes to ghouls, zombies, or haunted scarecrows—you can count me out. We'll cross the Rigby place off the list. There are other houses to steal from Buzzy Lennon."

I stood up to leave. "Does Buzzy know about your leaf-raking business?"

"It's not a secret," Daniel answered. "Our posters are all over town. Why?"

"Well, I doubt Buzzy's happy about it." I turned the doorknob. "The thing is, your posters aren't all over town. Not anymore. *Somebody*'s been ripping them down—and I doubt it was a scarecrow."

Chapter 7

Back to School

On the school bus Monday morning, I handed Mila a note. It read:

EM RETFA DESAHC
DNA EVILA EMAC
WORCERACS A YRROS

Like most codes, it looked hard at first. It was called a Double Backward Code. I invented it myself. First, I wrote the letters for each word in reverse order. Then I put all the words in reverse order. Instead of THE CAT ATE, it would be ETA TAC EHT.

Easy, actually.

Mila read the code, thought for a few minutes, then ran a finger across her nose. That was our secret signal. She got it. She slipped the paper into her mouth.

And swallowed.

We always destroyed our secret codes after reading them. That way, they stayed a secret!

"You're forgiven," Mila whispered. "You're also silly."

I found Kim talking with Danika and Geetha outside the main doors of school.

I gave her the necklace and three dollars.

"What's this?" Kim asked, holding the money.

"Strangest case I've ever worked on," I said. "The necklace was already there. So I kept the money. It's yours."

Kim waved it away. "No, it's yours. You earned it, Jigsaw."

The bell rang. We walked to room 201. We loved our teacher, Ms. Gleason. She was the nicest teacher in school. Maybe the smartest, too. Ms. Gleason believed in reading books aloud to us, even though we could do it ourselves. I liked that. It was relaxing.

We had art with Mr. Manus on Mondays. We were making leaf place mats. First we gathered leaves outside. Then we glued them to poster board. Mr. Manus was going to laminate them later that afternoon.

I finished first. With the extra time, I sketched a quick picture of the scarecrow in my journal.

Bigs Maloney looked over my shoulder.

Bigs had paint all over his smock, face, hair, and hands. "Needs blood," Bigs suggested.

I disagreed. "No, there wasn't any blood."

"What are you talking about?" Bigs asked. He jabbed a thick finger at the scarecrow. "This ain't real, is it?"

"It is," I answered. I told him the story. At recess, Bigs made me tell it all over again.

This time I sat on the tire swing, surrounded by an eager crowd of listeners.

"No way," Bobby Solofsky sneered. "He's making it up."

"I believe Jigsaw," Joey Pignattano declared. "He wouldn't lie."

"Stuff like that totally happens all the time," Athena Lorenzo offered. "Scarecrows *can* be haunted, just like anything. I read about it in a book once."

"What kind of book?" Mila asked. "A fairy tale?"

"No, a *real* book with real pictures of real ghosts and UFOs and aliens," Athena answered. "It was called, um, I don't know, like, *Freaky Things That Live*, or something like that."

"Athena's right," Lucy Hiller agreed. "Strange things happen all the time. The world is full of mysteries. No one can explain why."

"Yeah," Ralphie Jordan joined in. "Check out my socks." Ralphie slid up his pant legs. He wore a striped green sock on one foot and a bright orange sock on the other foot. "Beats me how that happened," Ralphie said, cracking a smile. "The world is full of mysteries!"

"The funny thing is," he added, "I've got another pair just like 'em at home!"

Chapter 8

Case Closed

I *should* have been happy. Kim Lewis had her necklace. Mila and I were paid. The case was closed.

But it felt like I had a swarm of bees buzzing through my brain. *Questions, questions, questions.* But no answers. I slid across from Mila in the cafeteria. "This case is all wrong," I confided.

Mila looked at me thoughtfully. She tapped a tooth with a long pink fingernail. *Click, click.* "We never solved the mystery," she stated.

Mila was right. We never did find out WHO stole Kim's necklace. Or, for that matter, WHY. I mean, why steal it, then return the necklace without getting a ransom? It didn't make any sense.

I scratched the back of my neck. "Got any bright ideas?"

Mila pushed aside her lunch tray. "Maybe the robbers weren't after ransom money after all. Maybe they wanted something else. Describe the scarecrow again."

"What's that got to do with anything?" I grumbled.

"Maybe nothing," Mila replied. "But tell me anyway."

"I thought you didn't believe me."

Mila thought for a moment. "Let's just say that the world is full of mysteries."

I frowned.

Mila continued, "I've got to treat you like any other witness, Jigsaw. Remember, it was

dark. And you were *frightened*. How well did you *really* see that scarecrow?"

"I didn't stop to take a picture, if that's what you mean. But I'm telling you, Mila. I saw what I saw. That scarecrow walked."

"Do you remember any details?" Mila asked.

I shrugged. "Flannel shirt, blue jeans, heavy black shoes. It walked stiffly, like a zombie."

"Let's go there after school," Mila suggested. "I want another look at that scarecrow."

That afternoon in class we studied Eddie Becker's all-time favorite subject—money! Ms. Gleason set out a bunch of food items, like cans and cereal boxes and other stuff. Each item had a different price. Then Ms. Gleason gave us all play money. We were allowed to buy anything we wanted.

The trick was we took turns being the storekeeper. We all had to figure out how to

make the right change. Ms. Gleason joked, "This will be good practice when we all become millionaires one day!" Pretty soon, we were all imagining what we'd really buy if we were millionaires.

"A superpowered telescope," Jasper Noonan announced. "So I could see all the way to Neptune!"

"My own karaoke machine!" Helen Zuckerman shouted.

"A roomful of art supplies," Geetha Nair confessed.

I knew what I'd buy: a clue. The stolen necklace was still a mystery. Who took it? Why did they take it? And why did they want *me* to deliver the money?

I got my lucky break that very afternoon. I was in line for the bus. A few kids were jostling around, bumping and yapping. Bobby Solofsky was pushing, like always. I asked Mila, "How'd you get home yesterday anyway? Did your father give you a lift?"

"Actually, Kayla's boyfriend stopped by right after you called," Mila said. "He gave me a ride on his mountain bike."

"Cool."

"He talked nonstop," Mila continued. "He said he took his bike everywhere—off trail or to school, it didn't matter. He teased me for riding the Big Yellow Twinkie."

I raised an eyebrow. "The Big Yellow . . . *what*?"

"Twinkie," Mila confirmed. "That's what he calls the school bus! Funny, isn't it?"

Mila continued enthusiastically, "You should have seen his bike, Jigsaw. It was a Schwinn Moab 3, with twenty-four speeds! A Cro-Moly frame, front suspension, grabber seat, the works."

It sounded strangely familiar. Then it hit me. I'd seen that bike before, in Kim Lewis's backyard. "White frame, red forks?" I asked.

Mila nodded. "Yeah, how'd you know?"

I ignored Mila's question. Instead, I asked one of my own: "Does this kid have a name?"

"Yeah, let me think, it was a strange name . . ." Mila squeezed her eyes shut, trying to remember. "Um, Fuzzy, or Wuzzy, or Buzzy. Yeah, that's it, Buzzy." She chuckled. "Goofy, huh?"

Chapter 9

The Rigby Place

As a kid, I loved connect-the-dots. You drew a line from one dot to the next. Then another. Then another. Almost magically, a picture appeared.

Detective work was the same thing. One clue led to the next. And the next. With Mila's new fact, I drew a line from Kayla Lewis . . . to Buzzy Lennon.

A picture was coming into focus.

I reviewed the facts of the case. Kim said it was a boy's voice on the phone. Mila heard a girl giggling in the background. Could it have been Buzzy and Kayla?

I tested my idea on Mila as we rode our bikes to the Rigby place. "Interesting," she said.

I gestured angrily at another shredded poster. "Look at that," I complained, pointing to the ripped bits of paper. "All of my brothers' signs have been torn down. How are they going to get any business?"

"Do you think Buzzy is behind it?" Mila asked.

Yes, I thought, *Buzzy Lennon might be behind* a lot *of things*. We arrived in front of the Rigby house. "Let's take a closer look at this scarecrow," Mila said, leaping off her bike.

The scarecrow was ordinary in every way. Just a bunch of leaves. Gloves for hands. The legs were tied with string to keep the leaves from falling out.

"A lot of footprints around here," Mila noted.

The dirt surrounding the bushes had been walked on recently. I put my sneaker beside the footprint. Whoever made the footprints had big feet. "Well, we know these prints weren't made by him." I pointed at the scarecrow. "Look. No feet."

Next I examined the scarecrow with my magnifying glass. A pattern of dirt smudges ran along the side of the scarecrow.

"It looks like it's been lying in the dirt," Mila said. "Like someone had stuffed it underneath the bushes."

"Now who would do that?" I wondered. "And why?"

Suddenly, Mila slapped her forehead and exclaimed, "How could I be so dumb!" She reached behind the scarecrow and fumbled with the shirt collar. "My stepmom is super tidy. She organizes everything. She even writes my name in the back of all my clothes with permanent marker."

She smiled triumphantly. "Look."

I craned my neck to read the label. "We're looking for a kid named Ralph Lauren," I said.

"That's the clothing label!" Mila said. "Read the other name!"

I read the name that was printed in black marker:

BUZZY LENNON

I looked up into the trees. There were hardly any leaves left. The sky was crisp and bright. Halloween was next week, then Thanksgiving, then the frozen days and lonely nights of winter. I turned to the front door of the sad, old, silent house. "Let's see if the doorbell works," I said.

The door slowly opened with an eerie squeak. Mrs. Rigby's small, red-rimmed eyes blinked in the sun.

"Yes, what is it?" she asked.

Chapter 10

The Final Piece

There was nothing remarkable about Mrs. Eleanor Rigby. There were probably ladies like her all over town. She lived alone in a big old house. She had white hair. She wore a pink sweater with large white buttons. Her right arm, I noticed, trembled nervously.

And she smelled of butterscotch.

The smell reminded me of Grams. But my Grams was different. She had us—my parents, my sister, my brothers, and me.

Who did Mrs. Rigby have?

Who looked out for her?

She told us that Buzzy Lennon gave her the scarecrow. "He just brought it over one day," Mrs. Rigby recalled, still puzzled by it. "He said I needed one. What a nice boy."

I exchanged looks with Mila. We were thinking the same thing. Of course, Buzzy brought it over. It was part of his plan to scare away the competition.

I asked if she needed help raking the yard. Mrs. Rigby apologized. She had already hired Buzzy to rake it next Saturday. "I'm too old to do it myself anymore," she admitted. She winked at Mila and me. "I have advice for you kiddies: Don't get old."

Mrs. Rigby gazed past our shoulders. "Though it's a shame to rake them up, isn't it? The leaves, I mean," she mused. "So beautiful, like a rainbow falling from the sky. The reds and oranges, the golds and burnished browns."

We thanked her and moved on. Our train had one last stop on the line. Kayla Lewis opened the door. She seemed startled to see us. "Jigsaw Jones! What are you doing here?"

"Stirring up trouble, like usual," I grunted. "Kim here?"

We found Kim in her basement. She was lying on the floor, finishing a jigsaw puzzle. A rounded border, 750 pieces at least. I

was impressed. It was called "Animals of Antarctica."

I studied the notes in my detective journal:

> ## THE CASE OF THE HAUNTED SCARECROW
> ## THE MOTIVE?
> ## GREED!!!

Kim smiled up at us warmly. "This is a nice surprise."

I wasn't so sure about that. I pulled off my cap and raked five fingers through my hair. "We never figured out who stole your necklace," I told her. "It's been bothering us. Like a puzzle that's not finished." I picked up a piece of a penguin's bill, pondered for a moment, then fit it into the puzzle.

I looked into Kim's eyes. They were blue, like the swimming pool at the YMCA. "I think we've been used," I said. "You and me both."

"Used? By whom?!" Kim asked.

"Buzzy Lennon," I answered.

"And your sister Kayla, I'm afraid," Mila added. "She's probably in on it, too."

Kim didn't look shocked. Maybe she suspected Kayla all along. "I'll start from the beginning," I said, glancing at my notebook.

"First, your necklace turns up missing. You don't know what to do. But your sister Kayla does. She suggests you hire me. She's in my brother Daniel's class so she zings him a text. Problem is, Kayla doesn't know me from a lumberjack. Why'd she pick me?"

Kim didn't answer. But I could tell I had her full attention.

"Then came the ransom," I continued. "They wanted *me* to make the drop-off. They wanted me outside in the dark of night, standing close—but not too close—to the Rigby place."

Kim blinked, concentrating on every word. "Do you get it now, Kim?" I said. "They didn't want ransom money. They wanted a *witness*. They wanted me to *see* something: a haunted scarecrow."

I sighed. "They played me like a cheap kazoo. Buzzy knew I'd get spooked. He knew I'd tell my brothers Daniel and Nick. Now, this is the important part, Kim, so listen close. See, my brothers just got started in the leaf-raking trade. Their rates are cheap. They wanted to take away some of Buzzy Lennon's business.

"You know Buzzy, right? He's Kayla's boyfriend. He was here the day you called me. I noticed his bike stashed in your backyard."

I suddenly felt tired of listening to my own voice. But I was nearing the end. And Kim seemed to be hanging on every word. "The plan worked perfectly," I said. "At my urging,

Daniel and Nick decided to stay away from the Rigby house, even though she pays a hundred balloons for a fall cleanup."

"There was no haunted scarecrow," Mila concluded. "It was Buzzy Lennon dressed up like one."

Chapter 11

A Gift of Autumn

Kim's fingers went to her throat. I noticed, for the first time, that she was wearing the necklace. "But . . ."

"The necklace never mattered," Mila explained. "It was a phony crime to get Jigsaw over there. It must have been easy for Kayla to take it. Your room isn't exactly Fort Knox."

Kim looked at me blankly.

"Fort Knox," I said. "It's where our government keeps the gold."

"It's been a two-person job all along," Mila said. "Buzzy and Kayla, together."

Kim had heard enough. Her face turned hard, angry. "What about Buzzy and Kayla?" Kim asked. "We can't let them get away with this."

"We'll fix them," I said. "I've got a plan."

Carrying rakes and garden tools, we showed up at Mrs. Rigby's house early

Saturday morning. There was a whole gang of us. Me, Mila, Daniel, and Nick. Kim came, too. So did Bigs, Ralphie, and Danika.

"Oh dear. This must be a mixup," Mrs. Rigby fretted. "Buzzy is supposed to be here at noon."

We giggled happily. Daniel, in particular, snorted with glee. I smiled. "Don't worry," I assured Mrs. Rigby. "You are this year's lucky winner. We're going to rake your yard for free!"

"Free?" she repeated. "But . . . won't Buzzy be upset?"

Nick's head bobbed up and down happily. "We certainly hope so!"

Daniel stepped forward. "What he means is, er, Buzzy will be upset that he couldn't be here to help."

"And, um, one more thing," I said to Mrs. Rigby. "I have a present for you." I pulled the artwork from my backpack. It was the leaf place mat I'd made in art class. "Now you'll be able to look at leaves all year long."

Mrs. Rigby looked at it for a long time, touching it lightly with the tips of her fingers. "It's lovely," she said, "the reds and oranges. The golds and browns."

"Like a rainbow falling from the sky," Mila said.

"Let's get to work!" Daniel shouted. "I want this yard done before lunchtime. I can't *wait* to see the expression on Buzzy's face when he shows up!"

It was worth the wait, too. Because Buzzy showed up right on time, at noon exactly. Too bad our work was already done.

Buzzy climbed off his Moab 3 bicycle. I

noticed, for the first time, that he wore heavy black shoes. Just like a certain scarecrow I knew. Buzzy looked at us in confusion. He stammered, "What the . . . ?"

"Hey, Buzzy, old pal!" Daniel teased. "You missed all the fun!"

Buzzy's ears twitched with anger. "What are all you creeps doing here? The Rigby house was *my* job."

"That's right," Nicholas replied. "It *was* your job—not anymore. You're living in the past tense, Buzzy old boy."

Buzzy Lennon sneered. His hands hardened into fists.

Mrs. Rigby appeared at the front door. She was carrying a tray. It held a pitcher of grape juice and a stack of paper cups. She looked up. "Oh, hello, Buzzy," she said.

"Er, uh, hi, Mrs. Rigby," Buzzy mumbled.

I stepped forward. "We were just telling Mrs. Rigby what a swell guy you were," I told Buzzy. "It was awfully nice of you to let us do her yard . . . for free."

"For FREE?!" Buzzy exclaimed.

"For free," Mila repeated.

Buzzy stared hard at me. I felt Nicholas and Daniel move closer to me—side by side by side. I spoke softly, so Mrs. Rigby couldn't hear. "Fair is fair, Buzzy—and you're foul by a mile. You tried to pull a fast one with that phony scarecrow. But you messed with the wrong guy. Now the trick's on you. It's time to hit the road."

"Yeah," Kim said. "Just dry up and blow away."

Buzzy glanced up at Mrs. Rigby, standing by the porch. He knew he couldn't make a fuss. Buzzy glanced at the scarecrow and the long line of leaf bags. He muttered and sighed. Without another word, Buzzy climbed back on his bicycle and rode away.

It didn't exactly break my heart to see him go.

I took a long, deep slug of grape juice. "Delicious," I told Mrs. Rigby. "Thanks."

"Oh no," Mrs. Rigby replied. "Thank *you*. Thank all of you. Please come and visit again sometime."

"We will," Mila said.

"Yeah," I agreed. "Especially if you've got more grape juice!"

Mrs. Rigby smiled happily.

Now, I'm not an expert when it comes to money. Sure, we study it in school. And I know whose picture is on the five-dollar bill. But right then, looking at Mrs. Rigby's face, I figured that her smile was worth a hundred dollars, easy.

Some days, being a detective is just about the best job you can get. The pay may not be so great. But the smiles . . . well, the smiles are priceless.

And the grape juice is free!

Read on for a special sneak peek at
a brand-new, never-before-published
JIGSAW JONES MYSTERY:

The Case of the
Hat Burglar

"Highly recommended."—*School Library Journal*
on *Jigsaw Jones: The Case from Outer Space*

It's their toughest case yet . . . Will this be the first
mystery Jigsaw Jones and Mila *can't* solve?

Our Toughest Case

It reads "Theodore Jones" on my birth certificate. But, please, do me a favor. Don't call me that. My real name is Jigsaw.

Jigsaw Jones.

The way I see it, people should be able to make up their own names. After all, we're the ones who are stuck with them all our lives. Right? I get it. Our parents had to call us something when we were little—like "Biff" or "Rocko" or "Hey You!" But by age six, we should be allowed to name ourselves.

So I did. I took Jigsaw and tossed "Theodore" into the dumpster. These days, only two people call me Theodore. My mother, when she's unhappy. And my classmate Bobby Solofsky, when he wants to be annoying. Which is pretty much all the time. Bobby is a pain in my neck. Let me put it this way. Have you ever stepped on a Lego with your bare feet? There you are, cozy and sleepy, shuffling down the hallway in your pajamas, when suddenly—YOWZA!—you feel a stabbing pain in your foot.

What happened?

The Lego happened, that's what.

In my world, that Lego is named Bobby Solofsky.

And I'm the foot that stepped on it.

So, please, call me Jigsaw. After all, it's the name on the card.

NEED A MYSTERY SOLVED?

Call **Jigsaw Jones**
or **Mila Yeh**,
Private Eyes!

Mila is my partner and my best friend on the planet. I trust her 100 percent. Together, we make a pretty good team. We solve mysteries: lost bicycles, creepy scarecrows, surprise visitors from outer space, you name it. Put a dollar in our pockets, and we'll solve the case. Sometimes we do it for free.

But the Hat Burglar had us stumped.

We were baffled, bewildered, and bamboozled. There was a thief in our school, and I couldn't catch him. Or her. Because you never know about thieves. It could be anybody—he, she, or even it. That's true. *It happens*. We once caught a ferret red-handed. Or red-footed. Or red-pawed. Whatever! Point is, the ferret did it. But in this case, no matter what Mila and I tried, nothing worked. The mystery stayed a mystery. It was our toughest case yet. And by the end, the solution very nearly broke my heart.

But let me back up a bit. It all began last week, on a frosty Tuesday afternoon . . .

Frozen

It was the coldest day of the year. Three degrees below zero. In other words, it felt like the planet Hoth from *Star Wars*. Or Canada, maybe. Even worse, there wasn't a single snowflake on the ground. Just cold wind and frozen skies. It was so nasty my dog, Rags, didn't want to go outside. And Rags *lives* for going outside. That morning, he stood by the open door, cold wind blasting his nose, and whined. "Sorry, Rags," my father insisted. "I don't like it any more than you do. But we gotta go."

Rags put on the brakes.

Eventually, my father talked Rags into it. I think he promised a treat. Looking outside, I felt the same way. I didn't want to leave my toasty house, either. But when my mother said, "Time for the bus, Jigsaw, no dillydallying," I had no choice.

My mother lets me dilly. And she lets me dally. But I can never dillydally. That's going too far. Not when there's a bus to catch.

At the bus stop, several kids stood together like a bunch of Popsicles in a freezer. I knew that two of them were Mila and Joey Pignattano, but it was hard to tell who was

who. Almost everyone was bundled in thick winter clothes, hats pulled down to their eyeballs. "Murfle, murfle," somebody mumbled to me through a wool scarf. I murfled back.

The wind snarled as if it were a snaggletoothed wolf.

Once the bus dropped us at school, we headed for our classrooms. Geetha Nair walked into room 201, dressed in a long colorful scarf wrapped around (and around!) her neck and face. The only part of her head that showed through were two round, chocolate-brown eyes.

Helen Zuckerman burst through the door. "I can't feel my nose," she announced. "It's frozen solid. I could snap it off like an icicle."

Joey poked Helen's nose with a finger. "Yipes, you're right, Helen. It's colder than ice cream."

Bigs Maloney, in contrast, strolled in wearing shorts and a long-sleeve shirt. "No coat, Bigs?" Ms. Gleason asked.

"It's in my backpack," he explained. "Just in case."

"Bigs, it's below zero outside. When are you going to put on a pair of long pants?" Helen wondered.

The big lug shrugged. "I like shorts better. They let my knees breathe."

"I wish it would snow," curly haired Lucy Hiller muttered. "I don't mind the cold if there's snow. Then we could go sledding . . . or build snow forts . . . or—"

"Make snow pies!" Joey cried.

"What?" Mila swung her backpack around with one hand. It landed softly at the bottom of her cubby. "Seriously, Joey. Snow pies?"

"Yes," Joey replied. "Snow pies are delicious. Only one ingredient: fresh, white, delicious snow. Yum!"

Stringbean Noonan gasped and pointed at Mila's hands. "Look, it's so cold your fingers turned purple!"

Mila laughed. She wiggled her fingers. "It's only nail polish, Stringbean. I had them done at the mall with Geetha and my stepmom this weekend."

"Phew!" said Stringbean. He seemed relieved.

Athena Lorenzo staggered into the room. "My hair. It was wet when I left my house. Now it's frozen solid!"

"Oh, Athena. Don't you have a hat?" Ms. Gleason asked.

"I used to," Athena said. "I think I lost it in school yesterday."

"Well, that's a problem," Ms. Gleason said. "Hats keep heads warm. It's important protection in this weather. Athena, do you know where we keep our Lost and Found?"

Athena shrugged. "I guess I lost that, too."

Ms. Gleason looked at me. I gave her a nod to let her know that I knew. "Jigsaw, could you please accompany Athena to the Lost and Found?"

Thank you for reading this **FEIWEL AND FRIENDS** book.

The Friends who made

The Case of the

Haunted Scarecrow

possible are:

Jean Feiwel, Publisher

Liz Szabla, Associate Publisher

Rich Deas, Senior Creative Director

Holly West, Senior Editor

Anna Roberto, Senior Editor

Val Otarod, Associate Editor

Kat Brzozowski, Senior Editor

Alexei Esikoff, Senior Managing Editor

Raymond Ernesto Colón, Senior Production Manager

Anna Poon, Assistant Editor

Emily Settle, Assistant Editor

Erin Siu, Editorial Assistant

Patrick Collins, Creative Director

Taylor Pitts, Production Editor

Follow us on Facebook or visit us online at mackids.com.

OUR BOOKS ARE FRIENDS FOR LIFE.